The Day
the Teacher Went
BANANAS

The Day
the Teacher Went
BANANAS

by James Howe

illustrated by Lillian Hoban

A PUFFIN UNICORN

Text copyright © 1984 by James Howe
Illustrations copyright © 1984 by Lillian Hoban
Cover illustration copyright © 1995 by Lillian Hoban
All rights reserved

Unicorn is a registered trademark of Dutton Children's Books

Library of Congress number 84-1536
ISBN 0-14-054744-4

First published in the United States of America by
Dutton Children's Books, a division of
Penguin Books USA Inc., 1984

Printed in the U.S.A.
First Puffin Unicorn edition, 1987   COBE
14   15   16   17   18   19   20

for my mother

One day a new teacher arrived at our school.

We didn't know what to call him, because he wouldn't tell us his name. He just grunted a lot.

When it was time for arithmetic, he
showed us how to count on our toes.

And we learned a new way to write.

We went outside for science class.

Then we went back inside for lunch.
The teacher ate sixteen bananas.

"Tomorrow, let's bring bananas for
lunch," we all said, wanting to be
just like our new teacher.

Then we had art class. Our teacher
taught us how to work with clay.

And paper.

And paint.

Then we studied music.

Suddenly, Mr. Hornsby, the school principal, came into the room with another man.

"There has been a terrible mix-up," Mr. Hornsby said. "This isn't your new teacher. This is a gorilla."

The man with Mr. Hornsby said, "I am your new teacher. My name is Mr. Quackerbottom. I was sent to the zoo by mistake."

Sadly, we all waved good-bye
to the gorilla.

"Now," Mr. Quackerbottom said, "what have you learned today?"

We showed him.

"Why, this is awful!" Mr. Quackerbottom
cried. "You all belong in the zoo!"

And the next day, that's exactly where
we went...

... to have lunch with our
favorite teacher.